D1330335

This Walker book belongs to:

Splish, Splash, Ducky!

Lucy Cousins

WALKER BOOKS

AND SUBSIDIARIES

LONDON • BOSTON • SYDNEY • AUCKLAND

Hello, I am Ducky Duckling!

When I'm feeling happy
I say...

Quack,

Oh, goody, hooray!
It's raining today.
I'm going to find
my friends to play.

Drip, drip, drop,
I hop with frog.

Quack,
quack,
quack!

I like to squirm
with wriggly worm.

A hug for bug
and a hug for slug.

Into the pond
to play with the swans.

Quack,
quack,
quack!

Splash, splish,
I swim with fish.

We shake our feathers
in the rainy weather.

Drip, drop, plip, plop.
Rain is funny on your tummy.

Quack,
quack,
quack!

Squeak, squeak,
hide and seek.

Quack, quack, quack!

Oh, no!
The rain has stopped.

No more drips.
No more drops.

No more quacking,
I'm feeling sad.
I think I'll go
and see my dad.

Cheer up, Ducky,
here comes the sun.
Look at the butterflies
having fun.

We'll quack together
whatever the weather.
Hop on my back and…

QUACK,
QUACK, QUACK!

For Gabriel

First published 2018 by Walker Books Ltd
87 Vauxhall Walk, London SE11 5HJ

This edition published 2020

2 4 6 8 10 9 7 5 3 1

© 2020 Lucy Cousins

The right of Lucy Cousins to be identified as author/illustrator of this work has been
asserted by her in accordance with the Copyright, Designs and Patents Act 1988.

This book has been typeset in Futura.
Handlettering by Lucy Cousins.

Printed in China

British Library Cataloguing in Publication Data:
a catalogue record for this book is available from the British Library.

ISBN 978-1-4063-8408-6

www.walker.co.uk

Lucy Cousins

is the multi-award-winning creator of much-loved character Maisy. She has written and illustrated over 200 books and has sold over 37 million copies worldwide.

978-1-4063-3579-8

978-1-4063-7654-8

978-1-4063-3838-6

978-1-4063-4501-8

978-1-4063-2965-0

978-1-4063-5547-5

Available from all good booksellers.

www.walker.co.uk